W9-CCU-521

Disney • Pixar

Adapted by Diane Muldrow
Illustrated by the Disney Creative Development Storybook Art Staff

A GOLDEN BOOK • NEW YORK

Golden Books Publishing Company, Inc., New York, New York 10106

©1999 Disney. ©1999 Disney/Pixar. All rights reserved. Mr. Potato Head® is a registered trademark of Hasbro, Inc. Used with permission. ©Hasbro, Inc. All rights reserved. Slinky® Dog ©James Industries. Printed in the U.S.A. No part of this book may be reproduced or copied in any form without written permission from the publisher. GOLDEN BOOKS®, A GOLDEN BOOK®, A GOLDEN STORYBOOK™, G DESIGN®, and the distinctive gold spine are trademarks of Golden Books Publishing Company, Inc. Library of Congress Catalog Card Number: 99-66204   ISBN: 0-307-13254-4   A MCMXCIX   First Edition 1999

We'd be happy to answer your questions and hear your comments. Please call us toll free at 1-888-READ-2-ME (1-888-732-3263). Hours: 8 AM–8 PM EST, weekdays. US and Canada only.

"It's Cowboy Camp time!" shouted Andy. He picked up Woody, his favorite toy cowboy. Woody loved Cowboy Camp. It was that special weekend every summer when he and Andy went away together.
Before leaving, Andy played a game with Woody and Buzz Lightyear. But the game got too rough, and Woody's arm went *r-r-rip!*

There was no time for Andy to fix Woody's arm before leaving. So Andy decided to leave Woody at home.

Woody couldn't believe it! He watched sadly as Andy went off to camp . . . without him.

A few hours later, Andy's mom began setting out tables and boxes for a yard sale. Before Woody realized what was happening, Wheezy—a toy penguin who had lost his squeak—was taken outside to be sold.

With the help of Andy's puppy, Buster, Woody rode to the rescue, determined to save the squeakless penguin!

Woody was almost safely back in the house when his arm caused him to fall off Buster. A man at the yard sale picked him up. "I can't believe it!" the man said. "I found him! I found him! I'll give you $50 for this stuff," he said to Andy's mom.

"Sorry, he's not for sale," said Andy's mom. But when she wasn't looking, the man put Woody into the trunk of his car and drove off.

From Andy's room upstairs, Buzz Lightyear saw what was happening. He raced out the window to try and save Woody—but it was too late. He was able to get one clue, though—he saw the toynapper's license plate.

Woody soon found himself in a strange new place. The toynapper set him down and left.

"It's you! It's you!" said a cowgirl.

Woody saw that he was face-to-face with three Western toys—an old prospector, a cowgirl, and a horse.

"Our gang is finally back together," the cowgirl said happily.

"We've waited countless years for this day!" said the Prospector. Woody looked confused. He didn't know what they meant.

"You don't know who you are, do you?" the Prospector asked.

Woody noticed an old magazine with his picture on the cover. And an old TV in the apartment played *Woody's Roundup,* a 1950's TV program featuring the world's favorite cowboy, Sheriff Woody. His sidekicks were Jessie, the yodeling cowgirl; Stinky Pete, the Prospector; and Bullseye, the sharpest horse in the West.

Woody couldn't believe his eyes and ears. He was famous!

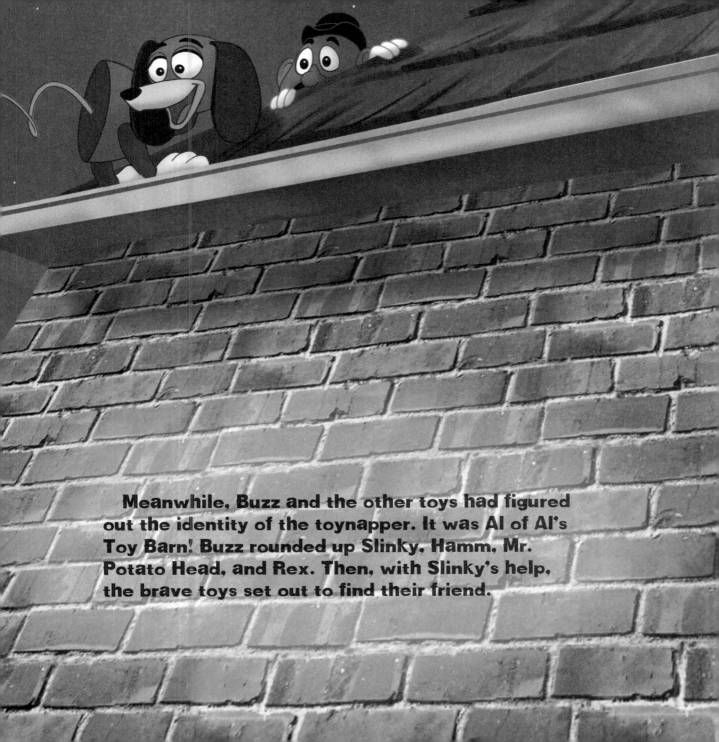

Meanwhile, Buzz and the other toys had figured out the identity of the toynapper. It was Al of Al's Toy Barn! Buzz rounded up Slinky, Hamm, Mr. Potato Head, and Rex. Then, with Slinky's help, the brave toys set out to find their friend.

Back at Al's apartment, Woody was having fun playing with his new friends. "Now we can go to the museum in Japan," said the Prospector. "Together, we're a complete set."

"Japan? I can't go to Japan," said Woody. "I've got to get back to Andy." Woody's arm was repaired and he was ready to leave. But before he left, he said goodbye to the Roundup Gang.

Then Jessie told Woody her story. She had an owner once who loved her—but grew up and gave Jessie away.

"Could Andy outgrow me one day?" thought Woody. He decided to stay with the *Woody's Roundup* gang after all.

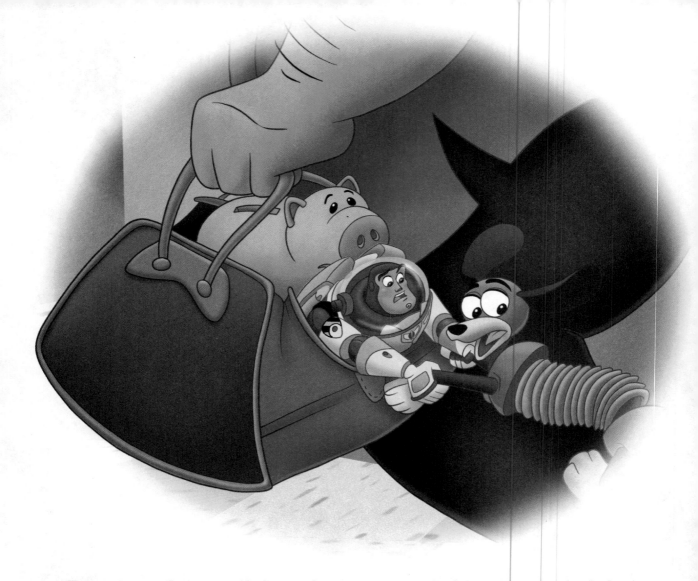

Just then, **Buzz** and the others were reaching the end of their long journey—**Al's Toy Barn.** The toys split up to look for Woody.

When they met up again in the back of the store, they found Al's office and snuck into his suitcase. Al never noticed them as he closed his bag and picked it up to leave.

Soon the toys found themselves in Al's apartment.
"We're here to rescue you," Buzz told him.
"You don't understand," said Woody. "Andy will outgrow me one day. This is my chance to last forever and be admired as part of a rare collection."

"YOU ARE A TOY!" Buzz shouted. But when he saw the look on Woody's face, he gave u "Let's go, everyone," he said sadly.

As Andy's toys turned to leave, Woody caught sight of something on television. The Woody on the TV was singing to a little boy on the screen. Suddenly Woody realized his mistake. He knew he belonged with Andy. Quickly he ran for the vent. But the Prospector blocked his way!

"You are not going!" said the Prospector. "I've waited too long for this and you are not ruining my plans."

When Al returned, he packed Woody and the other *Woody's Roundup* toys into a special carrying case and headed for the airport. He was going to take the toys to Japan to sell them to the museum! Andy's toys followed him. They jumped in an idling Pizza Planet Truck and reached the airport just minutes behind Al. Soon the toys were in the baggage loading area chasing after Al's carrying case.

Buzz found the carrying case traveling along a conveyor belt. The Prospector leapt out and started to fight Buzz. But working together, Woody and Buzz managed to stuff the Prospector into a child's backpack.

Meanwhile, Jessie was still in the case headed for the airplane! Acting fast, Woody chased the carrying case onto the plane and helped her out. When he opened the plane's escape hatch, the plane's wheels started to turn—with Jessie dangling right above them! Using his pullstring as a lasso, Woody swung down with Jessie just as Buzz and Bullseye galloped up to them. Woody and Jessie landed safely on Bullseye's back.

Together, the toys made it home just before Andy returned from Cowboy Camp. Andy was thrilled with the new toys and started making up games for them.

After their great adventure, Woody sure was glad to be back in Andy's room. As for Jessie and Bullseye, they were thrilled to be part of a family again.